# Tashlich
## at Turtle Rock

To Ruth Schnur,
Mom and Grandmom,
forever our centre that holds
– S.S. and A.S.-F.

For my beautiful daughter, Ruby, a
little gem and a genuine inspiration
– A.S.-M.

Text copyright © 2010 by Susan Schnur and Anna Schnur-Fishman
Illustrations copyright © 2010 by Lerner Publishing Group, Inc.

KAR-BEN Publishing
A division of Lerner Publishing Group, Inc.
241 First Avenue North
Minneapolis, MN 55401 U.S.A.
1-800-4KARBEN

Website address: www.karben.com

Library of Congress Cataloging-in-Publication Data

Schnur, Susan.
    Tashlich at Turtle Rock / by Susan Schnur and Anna Schnur–
    Fishman ; illustrated by Alex Steele–Morgan.
        p.   cm.
    Summary: Annie leads her family on a Rosh Hashanah hike to
    observe tashlich, where each person will ask God's forgiveness for
    the things they regret doing the previous year. Includes facts about
    this Jewish custom.
        ISBN 978–0–7613–4509–1 (lib. bdg. : alk. paper)
        [1. Tashlikh—Fiction. 2. Rosh ha–Shanah—Fiction.]
    I. Schnur–Fishman, Anna. II. Steele–Morgan, Alexandra, ill. III. Title.
    PZ7.S36442Tas  2010
    [E]—dc22                                      2009001871

Manufactured in the United States of America
1 — PC — 7/15/10

# Tashlich at Turtle Rock

BY Susan Schnur and Anna Schnur-Fishman

ILLUSTRATED BY Alex Steele-Morgan

KAR-BEN
PUBLISHING

"We always start at Old Log, Annie," Lincoln says,
giving me the look.

I give him one right back. "This year I'm in charge,"
I announce. "And this year we're starting at Turtle Rock."

It's the afternoon of Rosh Hashanah and we're on our way to do *tashlich*. That's when you go to a place with flowing water — a lake, a river, or creek — and you throw in pieces of bread that represent mistakes you've made in the last year. My friend Franny who lives in New York does it in the fountain at Lincoln Center, and my brother's friend Matt says he once did it in a toilet. My family has its own tradition.

"Is everything we need in your backpacks?"
Mom asks. "Apple?"
"Check!"
"Honey?"
"Check."
"Bread?"
"Check."
"I've got the pocketknife," Mom says.

"Follow me!" I say, leading them into the woods behind our house. This time of year the trail is lined with trees changing color. I've planned four stops along the way: Turtle Rock, Billy Goat's Bridge, Gypsy Landing, and finally Old Log.

"Okay, everyone!" I announce. "While you're walking, think of one really good thing you want to remember from last year." We hike quietly while everyone thinks.

When we get to Turtle Rock, I find four stones that can "write," and give one to each person.

"Okay. What good thing did you remember?"

Link goes first. He writes B-U-S on Turtle Rock. "I learned
how to ride the bus by myself," he says, "and it's really cool.
I can go anywhere!"

Then Dad gets up. He scratches the letters K-O-R-O-S-T-Y-S-H-E-V on the rock. "This year, Grandpa and I went to Ukraine. We visited the little village where he grew up. It's a trip that I'll always remember."

Mom goes next. She uses her stone to draw a picture of a lady with long hair. "I made a new friend this year," she says. She means Paula, who is also a writer. "We help each other write, read each other's work, and talk about books. I am so grateful for Paula."

When it's my turn, I can't decide between my bike and knitting.  Finally I draw a picture of my bike.  "This year, I learned to ride a two-wheeler," I say.  "Hooray!"

Then we stand up and look at what we've written. Together we shout, "AMEN!"

Dad scoops up some water from the gurgling creek
and splashes it over Turtle Rock to erase our writing.

"Take only pictures, leave only footprints,"
he reminds us.

"Our next stop is Billy Goat's Bridge," I announce.
"When we get there, find something that represents
what you want to 'throw away' from last year.
Start thinking!"

On the way to Billy Goat's Bridge we search the woods for
something to throw away.  By the time we get there, we each have
something in our hands.  We sit down and start explaining.
   Dad holds up an acorn cap that looks like a tiny mouth.
"I want to throw away saying bad things about people," he says.
   "You once said Mr. Frishberg looks like a frog," I remind him.
   "Exactly," Dad admits, as he throws the acorn cap over
the bridge.

Lincoln goes next. "I want to throw away being mad at Steven Pinker. He broke my calculator, but it was really an accident." Steven has red hair, so Lincoln throws a handful of red maple leaves into the water.

Then it's Mom's turn. "I want to get rid of the habit of saying 'yes' when I really mean 'no.' That's very hard for me. I'll agree to go to lunch with Abigail, when I really need to work." She throws a Y-shaped twig into the falls, and waves good-bye to "yes."

When it's my turn, I say, "I had a hard time making friends at camp last summer. I want to throw away being so shy." The rock I toss into the creek looks like a bunkhouse—well, to me, anyway.

There is one more thing to do before we leave Billy Goat's Bridge. I take out the bread and give everyone a chunk. Quietly, we break off little pieces and throw them into the water. These stand for private things that we feel sorry about, or want to get rid of in the New Year.

Then we stand up and look down at the waterfall. Together we shout, "AMEN!"

"On to Gypsy Landing," I announce. That's a big slab of rock on the other side of Billy Goat's Bridge.

When we get there, I tell everybody to think about one thing they promise to do in the coming year. While everyone's thinking, I gather some twigs and spell out the four numbers of the new Jewish year on the highest part of the rock.

"Now take off your shoes and socks," I tell them. "When you make your promise, dip one foot in the stream and make a footprint on the 'New Year' rock."

"I vow to put all our family photos into albums," Mom says,
dipping her foot in the cold stream.

"I promise to keep visiting Archie Meazle in the nursing home," Lincoln says, "even though my Bar Mitzvah project is officially over. His family lives in Mexico, so he never gets visitors."

"I vow to start making challah every Thursday night," Dad announces. He hops across Gypsy Landing on one foot and makes a footprint facing the new year.

When it's my turn, I put both feet into the water to make two wet prints. "I'm going to wake up early so I can get to school on time!"

Then we all stand up and look at our footprints. Together we shout, "AMEN!"

"Last stop is Old Log," I say. "Follow me!"

When we get there, Link empties his backpack. We all straddle fat
Old Log. Dad takes the pocketknife and cuts apple slices for everyone.
I open the jar of honey and we pass it around. Eating apples dipped in
honey symbolizes the sweetness of the Jewish New Year.

We recite a special tashlich prayer that Mom wrote.

"God, we have thrown out our mistakes and regrets,
And we have picked the best things from the year to keep with us.
Help us start over.
Help us remember our vows and promises,
And protect us this whole long year."

Then we all stand up and look at each other. Together we shout, "AMEN!"

## AUTHOR'S NOTE:

*Tashlich,* a Hebrew word meaning "you shall throw away," is a very simple ceremony that occurs on Rosh Hashanah, usually in the afternoon. People walk to streams or lakes (or in Jerusalem to wells) and shake out their pockets, pretending that the lint and crumbs are "sins" that they are tossing to the fishes. It's customary to recite these biblical verses (Micah 7:18-20): "Who is like you, God, who overlooks our transgressions? We know you will forgive us this year, as last, and help us throw our sins in the oceans!"

Since tashlich is so minimal but so powerful, our family has made up extra customs, as you can see. We have written this book so that your family has the confidence to add to tashlich, too -- songs, a real hike, and honest thoughts about yourselves at the New Year: what you're grateful for, what your last year was like, what you vow to do better in the months ahead.

Most congregations and families perform the tashlich ritual on the afternoon of Rosh Hashanah, but others do so during the period between Rosh Hashanah and Yom Kippur. Since the ceremony described in this book entails writing, if you don't write on Rosh Hashanah you may wish to do something else to recall your achievements during the year.

## ABOUT THE AUTHORS

**SUSAN SCHNUR** is a Reconstructionist rabbi whose "paper pulpit" is *Lilith Magazine,* a Jewish women's quarterly in New York City. She has written for many publications, including a weekly column for *The New York Times.* Susan lives with her husband in Boston, Massachusetts. She had a lot of fun writing this book with her daughter, **ANNA SCHNUR-FISHMAN,** a senior at Brown University. Anna loves linguistics, Yiddish, and writing.

## ABOUT THE ILLUSTRATOR

**ALEX STEELE-MORGAN** was born in Pembrokeshire, Wales, where she currently resides. Since graduating in illustration at the University of Plymouth, she has illustrated many children's books. Her favorite school subjects were art and science, a great combination for *Tashlich at Turtle Rock.*